I'm watching you, Persephone Hadley. I'm down here and I'm watching you. And later on tonight, when the time is right, I'll be paying you a little visit. Persephone Hadley – this is your life. Eighteen years old. Six months pregnant. The girl who killed my brother, the girl whose hands are awash with my brother's blood. Persephone Hadley. The girl who's going to die tonight…

A gripping continuation of the tale told in the award-winning NOUGHTS & CROSSES, which will be followed by a sequel to be published in Doubleday hardback in August 2003.

SPECIALLY PUBLISHED FOR WORLD BOOK DAY 2003

Praise for NOUGHTS & CROSSES:
From reviewers...

'Beautifully and believably written, you are gripped until the final pages where you arrive breathless and almost unable to take in the momentous ending' *Carousel*

'Possibly her best novel yet' *Children's Book News*

'Intelligent, emotional and imaginatively wicked... so well crafted that I insist on calling it a work of art' *Benjamin Zephaniah*

'A stimulating and provocative plot line that often leaves the reader chilled to the bone... written with the passion of an author who has a personal, chilling vision of the past, present and future' *Susan Harrison, Amazon.co.uk*

'In a world where black is white, Malorie Blackman forces us to think about race in a totally different and unusual way... a compelling modern tragedy' *Jackie Kay*

'Complex and challenging' *The Scotsman*

'A provocative read' *Daily Telegraph*

'A book which will linger in the mind long after it has been read' *Observer*

'Epic tome... dramatic, moving and brave' *Guardian*

'A sad, bleak, brutal novel that promotes empathy and understanding of the history of civil rights as it inverts truths about racial injustice... but this is also a novel about love, and inspires the reader to wish for a world that is not divided by colour or class' *Sunday Times*

'Flawlessly paced' *The Times*

'Startling and provocative... with its powerful theme of racial injustice, Noughts & Crosses engages the reader at a greater depth and in a more demanding way than any of Blackman's previous work. I read it in one sitting, reluctant to put it down, and so, I'm sure, will many young readers' *Books for Keeps*

And from readers…

'Intoxicating…the most gripping, stimulating and absorbing book I have ever read' *Sarah, Crowborough*

'The plot was so original, thrilling and gripping that I couldn't put it down until the last full stop' *reader in Norwich*

'You have inspired me to read again…Thank you!' *Leena, Hayes*

'You are an amazing author and your book…is the best book I have ever read' *Rebecca, South Wales*

'One of the best books I have ever read…every page was full of life and description…' *Aleshla, Fareham*

'This book is absolutely breathtaking. I only meant to start reading the first chapter but I became so engrossed I read it all!! The ending had me in tears and thinking about it now also does too' *reader in Cambridgeshire*

'An amazing and moving storyline…' *Ellie, Muswell Hill*

'You kept me so immersed in your book that I finished it in the space of last night and this morning!.. I just had to thank you for inspiring me' *Mona, Hounslow*

'I cried in three places and could not put the book down' *Jennifer, South Yorkshire*

'From the first page I was sucked in. I never wanted to put it down!' *Charlie, Northwood*

'This book made me laugh out loud in certain bits, made me tear two of the pages in my haste to turn the pages in certain bits and the end of the book made me cry. No book has ever done that before. The whole story was brilliant! There isn't a single bit that I thought was boring or had to skip over. And when I closed the book, I couldn't stop thinking about it. It's the best book I've ever read in my life' *13-year-old reader in Kent*

**Also available by Malorie Blackman,
and published by Doubleday/Corgi Books:**

A.N.T.I.D.O.T.E.
DANGEROUS REALITY
DEAD GORGEOUS
HACKER
NOUGHTS & CROSSES
PIG-HEART BOY
THIEF!

For junior readers,
published by Corgi Yearling Books:

OPERATION GADGETMAN!
WHIZZIWIG (available August 2003)

For beginner readers,
published by Corgi Pups Books:
SNOW DOG
SPACE RACE
THE MONSTER CRISP–GUZZLER

MALORIE BLACKMAN

An Eye for An Eye

Special publication for World Book Day 2003

CORGI BOOKS

AN EYE FOR AN EYE
A CORGI BOOK 0552 549258

Published in Great Britain by Corgi Books,
an imprint of Random House Children's Books

This edition first published specially for World Book Day 2003

1 3 5 7 9 10 8 6 4 2

Papers used by Random House Children's Books are natural, recyclable products
made from wood grown in sustainable forests. The manufacturing processes con-
form to the environmental regulations of the country of origin.

Corgi Books are published by Random House Children's Books,
61–63 Uxbridge Road, London W5 5SA,
a division of The Random House Group Ltd,
in Australia by Random House Australia (Pty) Ltd,
20 Alfred Street, Milsons Point, Sydney, NSW 2061, Australia,
in New Zealand by Random House New Zealand Ltd,
18 Poland Road, Glenfield, Auckland 10, New Zealand,
and in South Africa by Random House (Pty) Ltd,
Endulini, 5A Jubilee Road, Parktown 2193, South Africa

THE RANDOM HOUSE GROUP Limited Reg. No. 954009
www.**kids**at**randomhouse**.co.uk

A CIP catalogue record for this book is available from the British Library.

Printed and bound in Great Britain by
Bookmarque Ltd, Croydon, Surrey

for Neil and Lizzy,
with my love — as always!

An Eye for An Eye

one. Jude

It was winter late, winter cold, winter dark. A perfect February night. I kept the car in first gear as I snaked along, a couple of dozen metres behind the heavily pregnant girl I was following. The car lights were off and I was careful not to rev my engine. Just enough pressure on the accelerator to keep the engine ticking over. I couldn't be too careful. Even if she did glance back, the car's tinted windows would have rendered me almost invisible, but I hadn't lived this long by taking chances. And I didn't want the girl to know she had company. Not yet.

I watched the girl struggle onwards with two obviously heavy bags of shopping, one in either hand. Her footfall was tired and heavy, her shoulders slumped. Eyes narrowed, I watched her. Persephone Mira Hadley. The Cross girl who'd spun like a tornado through the lives of my family, leaving complete and utter devastation in her wake.

Sephy Hadley. The girl who was responsible for the death of my brother, Callum McGregor.

Sephy. Who, tonight, was going to pay.

An eye for an eye. A tooth for a tooth. A life for a life. A death for a death. It was that basic. It was that simple.

I pressed the appropriate button and the electronically controlled car window on my side slid down with barely a hiss. The chill night air stroked across my face and I welcomed it. The cold didn't bother me. In fact, the colder the better. I wanted everything around me to be frost and ice to match my mood, my unquenchable thirst for revenge. I'd waited weeks for this moment and I was determined to savour every second. I don't know who said that revenge was a dish best served cold but it was someone who knew exactly what they were talking about. A nought no doubt. It'd taken a lot of patience and planning, but now the moment I'd been waiting for since my brother's death had finally arrived.

I watched Sephy turn into the entrance of a building which had seen better days but not many worse ones. She walked up four worn, stone steps before carefully bending her knees but not her back to place her shopping at her feet, leaning the bags against her legs. I looked up at the shabby building. This block, this whole area was predominantly nought. The Crosses who lived around here were few and far between and were usually so-called liberals or bohemians, if they weren't simply too poor to find anywhere else to live. I wondered yet again why Sephy was slumming it in such a place instead of living like the spoilt little princess she was in the family mansion, surrounded by the family acres. There could only be one reason. Her mum and dad had obviously chucked her out when they had found out she was pregnant.

Was it the fact that she was pregnant or the fact that she was pregnant with the child of a nought that had got her booted out? Noughts and Crosses didn't mix, not if you didn't want a whole world of trouble. And certainly not if your surname was Hadley. Sephy's dad had survived his divorce from her mum and was even tipped to take over as leader of his party in the run up to the next general election. And he'd survived his divorce with its inevitable trip to the political wilderness by playing the 'them and us' card.

What was it he'd said in his last political broadcast?

'*All right-minded people in this country are concerned, and rightly so, about the flood of illegal immigrants entering this country.* (Cut to film footage of desperate noughts crammed into a small sailing boat, which looked like it was about to sink at any second.) *With the best will in the world, we simply cannot take the dispossessed of the world into our country. We have neither the space nor the resources. Crime figures are soaring* (cut to film footage of a nought man fighting against being handcuffed by two Cross police), *waiting lists for communal accommodation grow longer whilst illegal immigrants seem to jump the queue and get housed first — and enough is enough. We in the government are prepared to act and act now to stem the tide . . . blah . . . blah . . . blah . . . !*'

As a speech to stir up hatred between noughts and

Crosses, it couldn't be bettered. I take my hat off to his speechwriter. Just the right mix of indignation and emotive rhetoric. The '*flood*' of illegal noughts, the concern of the country's '*right-minded people*', the age-old 'if you're not for us, you're against us' gambit. Nothing like a good dose of racial hatred to get the juices flowing.

Sephy's dad. I hated him almost as much as I hated Sephy herself. Hate . . . What a ridiculously mild word. Much too sudsy a word to convey what I felt for Sephy. Hatred didn't even come close. It wasn't high enough or deep enough or wide enough or big enough to come anywhere near the feelings I had for my brother's killer.

'Hurry up!' I mouthed silently as I watched Sephy fish in her cavernous coat pockets for her keys. It took two deep delves into each pocket before she found them. She opened the front door, then bent at the knees again to pick up her shopping and enter the block of flats. I guess it's hard to bend with a belly bigger than a beach ball. I pulled up opposite the flats and turned off the engine just as Sephy closed the communal front door to the flats behind her. I used my mirrors to check up and down the street. Nice and easy does it. I wasn't attracting any undue attention. Good! In fact, the street was almost deserted. I looked up at Sephy's building. I knew she lived on the first floor. I knew the number of her flat. I knew her daily routine and her nightly habits. There wasn't much I didn't know about her. After she'd murdered my brother, her dad had made sure she had a police escort wherever she went, but that'd lasted less than a month. And she'd moved into her flat opposite within a week of killing my brother. I and my colleagues in the Liberation Militia make it our business to know about the lives and movements of all those in power and the people closest to them. We may not have vast numbers but we're very well organized and, what's more, the police and the government know it.

So, soon, would Sephy.

In less than a minute, a light came on at one of her windows on the first floor, like one eye of a lazy cat, opening. Sephy was in her flat. She was up there now and all alone. I watched Sephy's silhouette pass before the window as she closed the curtains.

Did she just look over in my direction?

Get a grip, Jude! She doesn't know you're out here. She doesn't know if you're alive or dead. She can't see you. Don't lose it now.

I'm watching you, Persephone Hadley. I'm down here and I'm watching you. And later on tonight, when the time is right, I'll be paying you a little visit. Persephone Hadley this is your life. Eighteen years old. Six months pregnant. The girl who killed my brother, the girl whose hands are awash with my brother's blood.

Persephone Hadley.

The girl who's going to die tonight.

two. Minerva

'Sephy, where've you been?'

I shivered. Sephy's flat wasn't much warmer than the hallway outside. I'd been sitting outside Sephy's flat for ages, freezing my bum off as well as getting some very suspicious looks from those passing.

'How did you get up here?' Sephy asked, closing the last of the curtains in her flat.

'I slipped past the front door downstairs when one of the other residents left the building,' I told her.

I didn't admit that I wasn't sure Sephy would let me in if I stayed on the street, ringing the doorbell to her flat. Standing in the hallway outside her own front door was something else though. I doubted that she'd keep me out – much as she might like to. I hadn't bargained for her being out though. Not on such a bitterly cold night. But I was wrong. So I'd sat down on the brown-stained, ill-fitting carpet in the hallway, with my coat tucked firmly around me and waited for my sister to get back.

The hallway on the first floor was dark and gloomy. No one could be bothered to splash out on anything more powerful than the odd forty-watt bulb by the look of it. In the dim light, the hallway walls looked mud-green, which probably explained a lot. Who'd want to see walls that colour in all their one hundred-watt glory? But even pitch darkness wouldn't've disguised the damp, dank smell, which permeated the very air in this place. When Sephy had finally trudged up the stairs and seen me seated outside her front door, she'd looked at me without saying a single word. Opening her door, she dumped her carrier bags on the sofa before she'd started closing all the curtains and whilst she hadn't exactly rushed at me with open arms, she hadn't kicked me down the communal staircase either. At least, not yet.

'I've been waiting outside your flat for over an hour. Where've you been?' It came out as an unintentional whine.

Sephy regarded me with cold, hard eyes. 'I've been shopping. What does it look like?'

I sighed inwardly. I hadn't meant to have a go the moment I set foot over Sephy's threshold. I tried again. 'You shouldn't be carrying heavy shopping in your condition.'

'I can't eat air, Minnie,' Sephy told me, heading for her tiny kitchenette.

The kitchenette was smaller than my bathroom at home. The whole flat was so small and poky, I couldn't've swung a mouse around without bashing its brains out at least twice. How could Sephy bear to live in a block like this? Apart from the fact that it was full of noughts, it'd have to fight its way up to be ruddy awful!

'What d'you want, Minnie?' Sephy asked. Her contemptuous tone told me that she knew how I felt about her flat. My expression must've given me away. She started unpacking her shopping, piling it on top of the tiny, tray-sized work surface before her.

'We wanted to know how you are?'

'We?' Sephy queried.

'Mother and me,' I said. 'We want you to come home.'

'Been there, done that, bought the T-shirt,' said Sephy. 'So, no thank you.'

'We're willing to put the past behind us,' I ventured. And the moment the words came out of my mouth, I knew I'd said the wrong thing. Sephy turned to me with a look of such venom that I actually winced.

'You're willing to put the past behind you . . .' Sephy repeated slowly. 'Which part of the past? My having a nought as my best friend? Or my having a nought as a lover? Or being kidnapped by him? Or getting pregnant by him? Which one of those are you prepared to forgive and forget?'

'Sephy, I didn't mean that the way it came out.'

'Of course you did,' Sephy dismissed.

'Look, Sephy, I'm trying OK. Give me a break.'

'Why should I?'

I sighed. Sephy and I had never been terribly close.

And God knows, I was doing my best to change that, but Sephy wasn't prepared to take a step towards me, never mind meeting me half way.

'I'll help you with that,' I offered, pointing at her shopping. I took one of the bags from her unresisting hands and started to pack up the tiny fridge. I mean, I've worn stockings that were higher than her fridge. Sephy's groceries consisted of a carton of economy orange juice, a two-litre carton of semi-skimmed milk, a small block of mature cheese, low-salt baked beans, half a dozen eggs, a bag of ready prepared salad (reduced) and a loaf of brown bread. That was it for the one food bag. The other bag contained household stuff which is just as well 'cause the fridge couldn't've held much more.

'Sephy, why don't you come home?' I tried again. 'You'd be more than welcome.'

'That's not what you all said when you found out I was pregnant with Callum's child,' said Sephy.

'That was then and this is now,' I told her whilst unpacking the second bag.

Sephy hardly heard me. She moved over to the living-room window and drew back one of the faded navy-blue curtains just a fraction but enough to peep past it. She let go of the curtain, turning to me as it fell back into place.

'You need to leave now,' Sephy said quietly.

'No. We want you home with us. Mother said I wasn't to take no for an answer this time.'

'And what did Dad say?'

'He has nothing to say about it one way or another,' I told her. 'It's Mother's house now, not his.'

'Have you seen him since their divorce?'

'Once.'

Sephy looked straight at me. 'Did he say anything about me?'

'No,' I lied.

And Sephy smiled. That's all. She smiled. We both knew I was lying. I'm so useless at lying.

'Aren't you going to ask how Mother's doing then?' I chided.

'No,' Sephy replied.

'Mother really misses you,' I tried, desperation beginning to creep into my voice. 'She's really upset that you haven't tried to contact her.'

'I've been a big let down all round, haven't I?' Sephy said seriously. 'A disappointment to Mother. An embarrassment to Dad. And both to you.'

'That's not true . . .' I began.

'Save it!' Sephy raised a hand to wave off my words. 'Next time you see Dad, tell him . . . tell him . . . Never mind. It doesn't matter.'

'He'll come round,' I said unhappily. 'Once he's had a chance to calm down and really think about things . . .'

'I don't care whether he calms down or not,' Sephy glared at me. 'You all think I should be the one begging for forgiveness, don't you? You all see yourselves as the ones who were wronged. It'd almost be funny if it wasn't so pathetic.'

'Sephy, that's not fair . . .' I began. I was putting my foot in it all over the place.

'Look Minnie, I don't want to discuss it,' Sephy interrupted. 'It doesn't matter any more. Nothing matters. You'd better go now. It's not safe for you to stay here.'

'Why not?' I asked, an unexpected chill trickling down my spine.

''Cause it isn't. Please leave.'

'How come it's safe for you then?'

'Minnie, do as I say and go before it's too late.'

I stared at my sister. 'You're scaring me,' I said at last. 'And I'm not leaving without you.'

'If you don't go now, you might not be able to leave at all.'

'I don't . . .'

There came a loud rap at the door. A strange look of resignation swept over Sephy's face and settled. The chill trickling down my spine was turning into a flood.

'Come here,' Sephy hissed, beckoning to me as she walked to the door.

Surprised by my sister's imperious tone, I did as she directed without a murmur.

'Listen. When I open this door, you must leave immediately. No questions, no conversation. Just go. Understand?'

I frowned, but nodded just the same. Sephy opened

the door. A vaguely familiar nought man stood in the doorway. He was tall and broad-shouldered and wore grubby, faded blue jeans, a navy-blue cable-knit jumper, a black jacket which seemed to be all pockets and a black woollen hat which hid most of his jet hair. So much so that it was hard to tell where the hat ended and his hair began. I scrutinized him, trying to figure out where I'd seen this guy before?

'Bye, Minerva,' Sephy said pointedly. She stood to one side to let me pass. You could've cut the sudden tension in the room with a spoon, never mind a knife. I looked from my sister to the stranger and back again.

'Bye, Minerva,' Sephy urged.

'I think I'll stay a bit longer.' I didn't even know I was going to say that until the words were out of my mouth.

'Yeah, let's all stay,' said the man. He strolled into the room, pulling the door out of Sephy's hand so that he could close it himself.

'Hey! You can't just barge in here!' I declared angrily.

The man's hand moved almost leisurely into his lower right-hand jacket pocket.

'Oh yes, I can,' the stranger disagreed. A heartbeat later, he removed his hand from his pocket and his fingers were now locked around the stock of an automatic gun, his index finger stroking up and down the trigger.

three. Jude

That shut her up. Stupid Cross cow. I hadn't expected Sephy's sister to be in the flat as well, but she was an added bonus – two for the price of one. That would really stick it to old man Hadley, wouldn't it? If he lost both his daughters in one fell swoop. The shocked, terrified look flashing over Minerva's face when she saw my gun was worth the price of admission alone. Sephy surprised me though – and I don't like surprises. No disbelief. No horror. No helpless, hopeless fear. Just a look on her face the likes of which I'd never seen before. It was like she was . . . glad inside. There was no trace of a smile on her face but she looked . . . lit up from within. That's the only way I can describe it. I frowned at her. I wanted her to be terrified. She wasn't even nervous.

And then Minerva started screaming. Stupid, stupid cow.

'SHUT UP!' I shouted.

She carried on shrieking. I wasn't going to tell her twice. I raised my arm ready to put her out of my misery, but Sephy stepped forward in an instant and slapped Minerva's face so hard, I'm surprised she didn't knock her sister's head clean off her shoulders. Even I flinched momentarily.

'Shut up, Minnie, or he'll kill you,' Sephy hissed.

Minnie choked down a sob, then bit down on her lip – hard, still staring at me like a frightened rabbit. This was how I wanted Sephy to look. The right emotion but on the face of the wrong sister.

'Let her go, Jude. She has nothing to do with this. It's me you want,' Sephy told me quietly.

'You know why I'm here then?'

'You've been following me for the last two or three days. It was obvious why.' Sephy shrugged. 'And I knew if I was right, you'd wait for today to make your move.'

She knew I'd been following her? Why hadn't she alerted her dad or the police?

Or maybe she had . . .

'Both of you – sit down on the sofa,' I ordered quickly, moving to one side of the front door.

Sephy turned to do as I commanded. Minerva was still staring at me. She obviously hadn't heard a word. Sephy grabbed her arm and pulled Minerva after her. I took a quick recce of the small flat, careful to keep my gun trained at Sephy and her sister as I looked around. We were alone, but for how long?

'I was expecting you this morning,' Sephy told me as I prowled around the flat.

'So you remembered what day this is?'

'Was there ever any chance of me forgetting?' Sephy replied.

I considered her. Once again she'd thrown me.

'Sephy . . .?' Minerva said her sister's name on a breath of bewilderment.

'Let her go, Jude. I won't give you any trouble, I promise,' said Sephy.

'I can't do that,' I said evenly. 'She knows who I am now.' I looked at Minerva and realized that until I'd said that, she still hadn't been sure.

'Jude McGregor . . .' she gasped.

Sephy shook her head at her sister's stupidity. I had to smile. The sheep that'd donated the wool for my hat was probably faster on the uptake.

'Sephy, why's he here? What's going on? Have you taken up with him now?'

Sephy turned to her sister with such a look of blazing contempt and loathing that I reckoned, if she'd had my gun in her hand at that moment, she'd've done half my job for me.

'I'm sorry. I don't know what I'm saying,' Minerva said quickly. 'I'm frightened. What's going on? Why's he here?'

'D'you want to tell her, or shall I?' Sephy challenged.

'You're the girl with all the answers. Why don't you enlighten us all?' The barrel of my gun was pointed straight at her heart and it was going to stay there until the job was done.

'Jude's here to kill me,' Sephy said, looking me straight in the eyes.

Minerva's eyes grew so round and huge at Sephy's words that they seemed to take over her entire face.

'W-why?' Minerva could hardly get the word out. 'Why now?'

Once again I was struck by the difference between the two sisters. 'Answer her question then,' I told Sephy.

Sephy studied me, her own expression strangely impassive. 'Because . . . today is Callum's birthday.'

four. Minerva

'*I know a place called Wrong-Is-Right*
  The sun will only shine at night . . .'

I turned my stricken gaze to my sister in disbelief.
She was *singing*. At a time like this she was singing. And
she was singing it all wrong. The nursery rhyme went,
'*I know a town called Right-Is-Wrong, Where birdies buzz
and bees have song!*' I shook my head. What on earth was
the matter with me? Jude McGregor was about to put
bullets through both of us and all I could think about
was a stupid nursery rhyme. I turned to Jude, afraid he
was going to shoot us just because my sister was singing.

'Are you prepared to let Minnie leave?' Sephy asked
him unexpectedly.

'I'm not going anywhere without you,' I told her at
once.

'Believe me, where I'm going you don't want to
follow,' Sephy told me, her eyes ablaze and burning
into mine.

And as I regarded my sister, I suddenly, inexplicably
felt dread – but it wasn't for Sephy, it was of her. She
looked so fierce – relentlessly so. I realized in that

moment, I didn't know my sister. I didn't know her at all. She was on one side of a galaxy-wide chasm and I was on the other.

Sephy turned back to Jude. 'How about it, Jude? Will you let her leave?'

'No can do.'

'Then tie her up and put her in my bedroom or the bathroom, but please don't harm her,' said Sephy.

'I can't do that either,' said Jude, total indifference in his voice. He took a step forward, his finger now firmly placed on the trigger.

'Wait. No, please. Wait.' I put out my hands as if to stop any travelling bullet in its tracks. 'Jude, wait. My dad will give you anything you want. Any amount of money. Or publicity. Or he'll release members of the Liberation Militia from prison. Just name it.'

There was no mistaking the absolute panic-stricken terror in my voice. But I didn't want to die.

I didn't want to die . . .

'How does it feel knowing you're living through your last moments on this earth?' Jude asked silkily.

I didn't answer. How could I answer?

'Now you know what my brother went through as they led him up to the scaffold to be hanged,' said Jude. 'I'm going to make you two suffer just as Callum did. Nothing too quick. No fast escape. Just slow, agonizing anticipation. I owe my brother that much.'

'Please,' I begged. 'Dad will give you anything . . .'

'There's only one thing I want . . .' Jude told me slowly.

'Name it,' I said. Adrenaline fuelled the relief coursing through my body.

'I want my brother back. Can your dad bring Callum back?'

I vomited. I vomited all over my lap and the floor. Panic, terror, adrenaline, relief, disappointment, despair – the cocktail of emotions churning inside me had to be released in some way. I puked my guts out.

Sephy stood up.

'Where the hell d'you think you're going?' Jude asked.

'To the bathroom to get some towels to clean up my sister,' Sephy told him as she made her way to the bathroom.

'You stay right where you are,' Jude ordered.

'Or what? You'll shoot me? You're going to do that anyway.' Sephy carried on towards the bathroom.

'Don't move!' Jude roared.

Sephy stopped. One more step, the slightest movement and my sister would get a bullet in her back. Everyone in the room knew that.

'Please,' I whispered. 'Sephy, I'm OK. Please.'

But I don't think she even heard me. She turned around slowly to directly face Jude.

'What're you so afraid of?' Sephy asked. 'I'm not going to run away or try to raise the alarm or do anything stupid. It's,' Sephy glanced down at her watch, 'it's just gone ten-thirty. As you've come here so late, I'm assuming you want to kill me just before midnight? That's what I'd do in your shoes. It's more symbolic that way. Callum didn't get to see this, his next birthday and I won't live past it either. If I were you, I'd shoot just a few seconds before midnight. It can be your present to Callum. Surely you can see the poetic justice in that?'

My heart was pounding so hard, I only just heard Sephy's words. But I heard enough. Sephy had no doubt that Jude would kill her. And if he killed her, I'd be next or first. Either way, I wouldn't be around to see the next sunrise. Images flashed through my mind of all the things I'd miss – Mum and Dad, my home, chocolate ice cream, smoked salmon, porridge. Stupid, stupid things. My stomach flipped over again. I swallowed down the saliva in my mouth, desperate not to be sick again. Desperate to just fade into the sofa and disappear until it was all over. Why didn't Sephy do something? Did she have a plan? Was she expecting company within the next hour and a half? Was she just trying to stall for time? Would Jude buy what she'd just said? Sephy was still standing so it looked as though he just might.

'So if we're going to wait out the next ninety-odd minutes,' Sephy continued. 'Would it hurt to let me clean up Minnie some?

'There's no point,' Jude said, his meaning ominously clear.

Sephy shrugged and made her way back to me. She fished into her pocket and handed me a couple of tissues before sitting down herself. I started mopping myself up.

'I just thought I'd do something about the smell, that's all,' said Sephy.

'I've smelt worse. I've lived in worse,' Jude replied.

Sephy nodded, her expression sombre. 'I'm sure you have.'

I couldn't take any more. I started crying. Semi-silent sobs which I had to fight with every gram of my strength to control. Jude could shoot us at any time. We might have one minute or ninety but they were finite and already counting down. Precious, precious minutes. I tried to brush the sick off my lap with the tissues but by now they were sodden. I tried to use the side of my hands to brush the mess onto the floor so that my whole hand didn't get covered in vomit. But I stank. The hot, sour smell of regurgitated pizza, Caesar salad and chocolate fudge cake was making me want to vomit again.

'*I know a town called Wrong-Is-Right,*
The sun will only shine at night,' my sister started to sing again.

'*Where up is down, and in is out,*
And when you want to whisper – SHOUT!
Where hate is right, and love is wrong . . .'

'You've got a good voice,' Jude told Sephy, surprising me.

Sephy shrugged. Then she grew very still and said, 'Callum always said so.'

I winced and drew back, mentally kicking Sephy for mentioning Callum's name. That was more likely to get us shot sooner rather than later. I hardly dared breathe as I waited for Jude's reaction, but he just stood there, his gun pointing at Sephy's heart, his unblinking gaze on Sephy's face. Silent moments turned into oppressive minutes and still no one spoke.

'I loved Callum, you know,' Sephy said unexpectedly. 'I still do.'

I stopped breathing altogether at that.

'You're a Cross. My brother is . . . was a nought. There's no such thing as love between noughts and Crosses,' Jude dismissed.

'Funny, but Callum once told me that too,' said Sephy.

'There you go then.'

'But he realized he was wrong. Very wrong. He told me so,' Sephy continued.

'And when did this so-called epiphany take place?' Jude sneered.

'In the cabin in the woods on the night you went to pick up the ransom money from my dad,' said Sephy, adding with a deliberate smile. 'The night Callum told me he loved me. The night Callum and I made love.'

Jude sprang to his feet. 'If Callum said that, it was only so you'd have sex with him. Callum never loved you. You're a ruddy liar.'

'No, I'm not. Callum loved me and I loved him and this pregnant bulge under my dress proves it,' Sephy said calmly.

I gasped, both with fear and to fill my aching lungs. But mainly with fear. Was Sephy deliberately trying to provoke him? If so, then she was succeeding.

'Callum didn't love you,' Jude said with scorn. 'He hated you Crosses almost as much as I do. Why d'you think he joined the Liberation Militia?'

'Desperation? Anger? Fear? I don't know,' said Sephy evenly. 'But Callum admitted to me that he'd got it wrong. He finally realized that your way of doing things will never work. Sooner or later, you and your kind will wake up to the fact that two wrongs don't make a right.'

'My kind . . .? Just what *kind* would that be?' Jude's voice had grown dangerously soft.

'Sephy, please don't antagonize him,' I begged, my hand on Sephy's arm.

She merely shrugged me off as she carried on talking. 'People like you who think it's OK to maim and kill to get what you want. People like you who think the end justifies the means. People like you who . . .'

'Enough!' Jude took a step forward.

'People like you who would kill your own brother's child rather than live and let live . . .'

'SHUT UP!' Jude pressed his gun against the centre of Sephy's forehead.

'No . . .' I whispered. A muscle twitching in Jude's

cheek was the only movement from his entire body.

'What's the matter, Jude? Are you jealous? Is that what this is about?' Sephy's eyes gleamed, a smile played across her face. She looked – almost happy. Wildly, ecstatically happy. 'Callum had his white nought hands all over my black Cross body . . . Imagine that, his tongue in my mouth, his body joined with mine whilst he whispered over and over again how much he loved me, how much he adored me, how I meant more to him than anyone in the world – including you. Especially you . . .'

'SEPHY, NO . . .' I screamed.

Jude pulled the trigger.

five. Jude

The gun jammed. I couldn't believe it. My gun jammed. It's never, ever done that on me before. My heart was racing so fast it sounded like a car engine in high gear. I was breathing so hard my chest was moving up and down like pistons in overdrive. I couldn't believe that Sephy had provoked me into losing my cool like that. I'm a trained Liberation Militia soldier. I've been interrogated by experts and they'd never got anything out of me, but Sephy had managed to get under my skin with just a few well chosen words. If I thought I hated her before, then this moment taught me that deep hatred can intensify and grow and feed on itself in a way that surprised even me.

My finger was on the trigger ready to try again – and again until the ruddy gun un-jammed. But then stupid cow Minerva leapt up like this was some kind of cheap TV soap and tried to force my arm up. Less than a second later, Sephy was also on her feet. Minerva was screaming and crying and struggling to keep my arm and the gun pointing at the ceiling, but she was losing. I'd take care of her first, then Sephy. I expected to feel

Sephy's hand on my arm as well, pushing it upwards, away from her, out of harm's way. But once again, Sephy surprised me. She was pulling her sister off me. And she succeeded because Minerva hadn't been expecting her sister's attack on her any more than I had.

Sephy pulled Minerva off me and threw her down onto the sofa, before spinning to face me.

'Go on, Jude. Do it. Shoot me,' Sephy urged. 'Go ahead. What're you waiting for? SHOOT ME.'

And I was about to do it too. I came that close. But my heart stopped racing and my mind took over again. I shook my head slowly as I realized at last just what was going on. When Sephy'd said she wouldn't try to escape or raise the alarm she'd meant every word. Every single word.

'You really want me to do it, don't you?' Stunned, I still couldn't quite believe it.

'You've been following me for days. I could've reported it and had you arrested at any time – but I didn't. You're only doing what we both want so get on with it,' Sephy told me.

'Sephy, no,' her sister whispered with shock.

'You shut up. Just shut up,' The mask was well and truly off now as Sephy whipped around to face her sister. 'I didn't want you here. I don't want you or any of my so-called family anywhere near me. I hate your guts and you're all too stupid to see that. I'll never forgive you, any of you, for the way you treated Callum and me. You all just stood by and let him die . . . And

I'm worse than all of you. I could've saved him but I didn't. I couldn't. And I can't live with that any more.'

Sephy buried her face in her hands, as her body just seemed to crumple. She fell to her knees, her whole body wracked with sobs of pain and anguish. My arm fell to my side as I stood before her, watching. And there we all were, like figures in a play who'd forgotten our next lines.

Sephy looked up at me, her eyes swimming with tears. 'So go ahead, Jude McGregor,' she said quietly. 'You owe it to your brother and you'd be doing me a favour. Consider it a *coup de grâce*, the one act of mercy in your whole, miserable life.'

'Sephy, what about your child?' Minerva asked. Her voice made me jump. I'd forgotten she was even there. 'Your child needs you.' Minerva continued. 'And it's Callum's child too.'

'But it's not Callum. Don't you get that yet? I could've saved Callum if I'd had an abortion – Dad made that crystal clear, but I couldn't do it.'

'Your father said *what*?' My blood ran ice-cold at Sephy's words.

'Dad wouldn't do that,' Minnie protested. 'You must've made a mistake . . .'

'Minerva, grow up,' said Sephy. 'One way or another, Dad has sacrificed all of us in his quest to get to the top. Can't you see that?'

And even if Minerva didn't believe her, I sure as hell did. Kamal Hadley could've saved my brother, but he didn't get his own way when it came to getting rid of his own grandchild, so he let my brother swing. He was just as responsible for Callum's death as the Cross scum before me.

'So you let my brother die . . .' I hissed.

'Yes, I did,' Sephy raised her head to look directly at me. 'So do what you came here to do. Don't wimp out.'

'No, Jude. Don't listen to her,' Minerva told me. 'She doesn't know what she's saying. Sephy and Callum had choices, but their baby didn't. Sephy had to choose the baby over everything and everyone else.'

'Including my brother?'

'Callum and I were never great friends, but I knew him well enough to know that he'd want his child to live,' Minerva whispered fearfully. 'And Sephy's carrying your nephew or niece. Are you really prepared to kill Callum's child just so that you can feel better?'

'I'm not doing this for me,' I told her.

'Then who is it for?' If Minerva thought she could appeal to my better nature then she was way off course. I didn't have one. 'Listen, Jude, killing Sephy won't bring Callum back. It won't make him rest easier in his grave. It won't be for anyone's benefit but your own.'

'You don't know what you're talking about?'

'Yes, I do,' Minerva shot straight back at me. 'You blame Sephy for Callum's death and you want revenge. Don't pretend it's for any other reason than to make you feel better. At least be honest about that.'

'And is that what we in the Liberation Militia are fighting for? To make ourselves feel better?'

Minerva regarded me, but wisely didn't answer.

'Go on then. You know so much about what I'm thinking and feeling, tell me why I joined the Liberation Militia?'

Silence.

'Answer me!' I roared at her.

'Why does anyone join a t-terrorist group . . . ?' Minerva began.

'We're not terrorists. We're freedom fighters,' I put her straight on that one.

'One man's meat is another man's poison?' Minerva replied, unable to keep the scathing note out of her voice. 'You bomb and kill innocent people . . .'

'And how many noughts are killed by Cross oppression? How many of us die mentally and physically from Cross abuse? But why should you care about that? As long as it doesn't directly affect you, you lot couldn't care less. None of you bothers to listen when we try to tell you how we feel, how it is. The only way we can get your attention is to shout. Shout hard and loud.'

'And bombing and killing is your way of shouting?' asked Minerva.

'It gets your attention.'

'It loses you all sympathy . . .'

'We don't want your ruddy sympathy,' I shouted at her. 'We want equality. We want the same rights and freedoms that you Crosses enjoy. *Stuff* sympathy.'

'My sister isn't your enemy,' Minerva told me. 'She tried to help Callum. She told anyone who would listen that Callum had done nothing wrong.'

'If it wasn't for her, my brother would be alive today. She murdered him . . .'

'He was hanged . . .'

'If she'd left him alone, Callum wouldn't've sought her out and got caught. He'd be alive right now.'

And there was absolutely nothing Minerva could say to that.

'Jude, no more talk. Just get it over with,' Sephy said wearily.

'Sephy, this isn't right,' Minerva immediately protested. 'Think of your child.'

'I've thought of nothing else,' Sephy cried. 'And with each second that passes, I hate this thing growing inside me more and more – because it's alive and Callum is dead and it should've been the other way around.'

'You don't mean that,' said Minerva.

'Minnie, leave me alone,' Sephy struggled to her feet. 'You always hated Callum, so why should you care what happens to any of us?'

'That's not fair. I do care,' said Minerva standing up.

'Just shut up a minute, both of you.' I'd had enough. I needed to get my head together and think.

I'd come here, ready, willing and able to kill Sephy and now that'd changed. And why? Because she *wanted* to die. If I killed her, all I'd be doing is putting her out of her misery. And I wasn't here to make things easier for her. But what then? What was my next move?

'You're not going to do it, are you?' Sephy said, watching me. 'Why? Are you bottling out? Would it help if I got down on my knees and begged you to do it? Or maybe I should get down on my knees and beg for my life. Is that what does it for you?'

'Sephy, shut up,' Minerva told her.

'Is that it, Jude?' Sephy kept pushing. 'Do you like your victims helpless and pleading? If that's what it takes, I'll do it.'

Minerva jumped up and stood in front of her sister. 'If you want to kill someone, then I'm right in front of you. But you will not hurt my sister and her baby. I swear on Callum's grave you won't.'

And then like a stupid, stupid cow, Minerva made a break for the door, screaming for help at the top of her lungs. So I did what I had to do. I raised my gun – and pulled the trigger. And this time, it didn't jam. This time it went off. Minerva hit the ground hard, twitched and was still.

six. Minerva

'MINERVA! Minnie, speak to me.'

I opened my eyes slowly. I was so cold. Why was I so cold? Sephy's face was above me and there were tears in her eyes. She had my head cradled on her lap. And above her stood . . . Jude. And then it all came crashing back to me. There'd been a bang – like a door being slammed. And something had exploded in my shoulder, like a rocket igniting under my skin and fizzing through me.

'Seph . . .?' I tried to speak but my lips seemed to be frozen together. When had it got so cold? Sephy moved my head quickly but gently and placed it down on the carpet before clambering to her feet.

'You murdering bastard!' she screamed.

'If I'd wanted to kill your sister, she'd be dead,' Jude replied.

'Are you going to kill her?'

'No.'

'Are you going to kill me?' asked Sephy.

'No. Not any more,' said Jude. 'Look at you. Daddy's kicked you out and you look three times your age. I reckon it'd hurt you more to stay alive.'

'My father didn't kick me out. I walked out. I didn't want to be anywhere near my family. It was my decision.'

''Course it was,' Jude derided.

I tried to open my mouth to tell Jude that it was true – every word, but I couldn't get my tongue to form the words. I attempted to sit up, but pain like a fiery arrow lanced through me and I collapsed back down onto the floor. And just like that the pain stopped and I felt ice cold again.

'If you're not going to kill us, then please let me phone for an ambulance,' said Sephy.

'Who's stopping you?' Jude told her.

I watched through half closed eyes as Sephy made her wary way to the phone. Her hand reached out for the telephone receiver, then hesitated.

'Go on then,' said Jude. 'No one else around here will do it for you. We noughts mind our own business. You Crosses have taught us that if nothing else.'

'I wanted to be left alone. That's why I moved in here,' said Sephy.

'If you say so.'

'I do say so,' said Sephy, adding deliberately. 'You see, I knew you would come after me.'

Jude and Sephy watched each other and I was forgotten. I was bleeding to death on the cold, hard floor and I was forgotten.

'Go ahead. Phone for your ambulance,' said Jude at

last. 'By all means make sure that one's on its way.'

Sephy pressed the keys to phone the emergency services. She turned to me and tried to smile reassuringly before she started talking into the phone, but I couldn't hear what she was saying and her voice was getting further and further away – and the room was receding with her. I realized I was passing out, but not before I saw Jude walk towards my sister, his gun raised. I tried to speak, I tried to warn her, and I tried to stay conscious. But my eyes closed . . .

seven. Jude

Minerva wouldn't be any more trouble. She was out of the game but she'd live. I'd seen enough bullet wounds in my time to know that much. I waited until Sephy put the phone down before placing my gun against her temple. She froze.

'You may not care about yourself, Persephone Hadley, but for all your big talk you do care about your sister and everyone else around you,' I said. 'And no matter how hard you try to convince me otherwise, we both know you care about that baby inside you.' I lowered my gun and replaced it with my lips against Sephy's temple, whispering silkily. 'And that's how I'll get my revenge on you, through your child.'

'You touch my child and I'll kill you. I swear I will,' Sephy pulled away and rounded on me like a mother lioness.

'Ah . . . not so different from me after all,' I smiled. 'And not so keen to die now either, I think.'

'Jude, you leave my child alone. I'm warning you,' said Sephy.

I smiled. Already an idea was forming.

'I'm going to ruin your life and the lives of everyone you care about, and your child is going to help me do it.'

Away in the distance, I could hear the sound of sirens getting closer. I looked around the flat, then back at Sephy. And at last I had what I'd come here for. For the first time since I'd entered the room, Sephy was afraid. Terrified. Her whole body shook with it. Yes, I did have a plan. It wasn't just talk. And it would take a lot of time, a lot of work and more patience than I'd ever needed before – but I would succeed. And my brother Callum would finally be avenged.

'Jude, leave us alone, please,' Sephy whispered.

I put the safety back on my automatic and shoved it into my pocket. I placed my hand against Sephy's stomach. She flinched but didn't step away. I felt a tremulous movement beneath my hand. The baby had obviously kicked.

'I'll be seeing you, Sephy,' I warned her. 'You and your child.'

And I left her flat as the sound of sirens rang out from beneath Sephy's window.

ABOUT THE AUTHOR

MALORIE BLACKMAN had a variety of jobs before turning to writing full time, including travelling within Europe and the United States when she worked as a Database Manager.

Her first book, *Not So Stupid!*, was a selected title for the 1991 Feminist Book Fortnight, and Malorie participated in the first BBC TV Black Women's Screenwriting Workshop in 1991. Her books for the Random House Children's Books lists include *Noughts & Crosses*, *Hacker*, *Thief!*, *A.N.T.I.D.O.T.E.*, *Dangerous Reality* and *Pig-Heart Boy*, which was shortlisted for the Carnegie Medal and adapted into a BAFTA winning BBC TV serial in 1999. Both *Hacker* and *Thief!* won the Young Telegraph/Gimme 5 Award – Malorie is the only author to have won this award twice! – and *Hacker* also won the W H Smith Mind-Boggling Books Award in 1994.

Her first book about Sephy and the world in which she lives was *Noughts & Crosses*, which was unanimously well reviewed and won the Children's Book Award of 2002, the Sheffield Children's Book Award and the Lancashire Children's Book Award.

Voted as Voice/Excelle Children's Writer of the Year in 1997, Malorie lives with her husband and daughter in Kent, along with a large collection of books – over 10,000 at the last count!

NOUGHTS & CROSSES
Malorie Blackman

Callum is a nought – a second-class citizen in a
world run by the ruling Crosses...

Sephy is a Cross, daughter of one of the most
powerful men in the country...

In their world, noughts and Crosses simply don't mix.
And as hostility turns to violence, can Callum and
Sephy possibly find a way to be together?
They are determined to try.

And then the bomb explodes...

A gripping, stimulating and totally absorbing novel
set in a world where black and white are right
and wrong.

'Will linger in the mind long after it has been read'
Observer

'An incredible novel that is as heart-rending
as it is provocative' *The Bookseller*

'Inspires the reader to wish for a world that is not
divided by colour or class' *The Sunday Times*

'Flawlessly paced' *The Times*

WINNER OF THE CHILDREN'S BOOK AWARD
WINNER OF THE SHEFFIELD CHILDREN'S
BOOK AWARD
WINNER OF THE LANCASHIRE CHILDREN'S
BOOK OF THE YEAR AWARD

ISBN 0 552 546321

A stunning and absorbing sequel to the award-winning
NOUGHTS & CROSSES, and
AN EYE FOR AN EYE...

KNIFE EDGE
Malorie Blackman

For fifteen years, Sephy – a singer – has struggled
to raise her mixed-race child in an apartheid society,
telling Callie Rose very little about her father,
and trying to make her mark in the entertainment
business – which is rife with its own prejudices.

But suddenly and dramatically, Callie discovers the
truth about her dual heritage – that her father, Callum,
was hanged for terrorism! Can mother and daughter
heal the rift that now opens between them? And can
Callie ignore the pain of the past as she takes her
own steps towards her future?

A riveting and page-turning novel that will confirm
Malorie Blackman's status as one of today's top
authors for young readers.

ISBN 0 385 60527 7

PIG-HEART BOY
Malorie Blackman

All I had to do was go downstairs. Or I could call Dad and tell him that I didn't want to meet Dr Bryce and that would be the end of that.   Life would go on as normal. And I'd be dead before my fourteenth birthday…

Cameron is thirteen and desperately in need of a heart transplant when a pioneering doctor approaches his family with a startling proposal. He can give Cameron a new heart – but not from a human donor. From a *pig*.

It's never been done before. It's experimental, risky and *very* controversial. But Cameron is fed up with ust sitting on the side of life, always watching and *never* doing. He *has* to try – to become the world's first pig-heart boy…

'A powerful story about friendship, loyalty and family around this topical and controversial issue'
Guardian

'Warm, well-packed story… Moving but never maudlin, this is a tale of courage stretched to the limit'
T.E.S.

**SHORTLISTED FOR THE CARNEGIE MEDAL
A BAFTA AWARD-WINNING TV SERIAL**

ISBN 0 552 528412

A.N.T.I.D.O.T.E.
Malorie Blackman

'The words exploded from me in a burst of white-hot anger.
'It's a lie.'

It's a normal Friday evening for Elliot – until the police knock on the door and tell him his mum's in serious trouble! A security video clearly shows her breaking into a giant pharmaceutical company on behalf of A.N.T.I.D.O.T.E., the environmental action group.

Elliot can hardly believe it. His mum's a secretary, isn't she? Not a SPY! And even worse – now she's gone on the run...

'Malorie Blackman has successfully rebooted the ripping yarn' *The Times*

'A gripping techno-thriller' *Independent On Sunday*

HIGHLY COMMENDED IN CATEGORY 1998
SHEFFIELD CHILDREN'S BOOK AWARD

WINNER OF THE STOCKPORT KEY STAGE 2
BOOK OF THE YEAR AWARD

ISBN 0 552 528390

HACKER
Malorie Blackman

MESSAGE: THIS IS THE SYSTEM OPERATOR.
WHO IS USING THIS ACCOUNT?
PLEASE IDENTIFY YOURSELF...

When Vicky's father is arrested, accused of stealing over
a million pounds from the bank where he works, she is
determined to prove his innocence. But *how*, when all
the evidence is hidden in computer files?

Helped by her brother Gib and his best friend Chaucy,
Vicky decides to hack into the bank's computers.
For if there is one school subject she is really good
at, it is computing. But even if she does manage to
break into the system, can she find the answers
before the real thief finds her?

'A fast-moving contemporary adventure' *School Librarian*

'Refreshingly new' *Weekend Telegraph*

WINNER OF THE 1994 W H SMITH
MIND-BOGGLING BOOKS AWARD,
THE YOUNG TELEGRAPH/GIMME 5 AWARD
FOR BEST CHILDREN'S BOOK OF THE YEAR
and the UKRA AWARD.

ISBN 0 552 527513

THIEF!
Malorie Blackman

Lydia's last thought before darkness closed over her mind was that the strange, swirling storm had trapped her. Would it ever let her go?

Fleeing onto the moors when she is unfairly accused of theft, an extraordinary storm suddenly whirls twelve-year-old Lydia into the future – a computer-dominated future where her home town is now ruled by a cruel tyrant. As Lydia struggles to get back to her own time, she discovers she must face a terrible confrontation...

'Spellbinding... must surely establish Malorie Blackman as one of today's outstandingly imaginative and convincing writers'
Junior Bookshelf

WINNER OF THE 1996 YOUNG
TELEGRAPH/FULLY BOOKED AWARD

ISBN 0 552 528080

DEAD GORGEOUS
Malorie Blackman

Life is tough for Nova. Her frantic parents are obsessed
by running their hotel and her older sister seems too
grown-up and good-looking to spend time with her
any more. Then Nova meets the gorgeous Liam
and things start to look up…

But Liam has problems of his own. He's permanently
stuck at the hotel and Nova's sister, the girl of
his dreams just looks straight through him – because
he's a ghost!

Could a new friendship between Nova and Liam help
them both see the light at the end of the tunnel?

A truly thought-provoking and entertaining black
comedy from the very talented Malorie Blackman.

'Blackman is known for her tightly plotted, fast
moving fiction' *Books for Keeps*

'Few writers can sustain a plot as well as Malorie
Blackman' *Sunday Telegraph*

'Blackman is becoming a bit of a national treasure'
The Times

ISBN 0 385 60009 7

DANGEROUS REALITY
Malorie Blackman

'This is the story of Mum's latest miracle – VIMS – and how it almost got me killed…

VIMS – the Virtual Interactive Mobile System – is the creation of Dominic's scientist mum. And it's *amazing*. An artificial intelligence masterpiece controlled by a single glove and a special pair of glasses, it can disarm a car bomb, search through underground pipes – or hold a baby…

But then VIMS attacks violently and without warning, and Dominic realizes it is no longer a fantastic game. It's a dangerous reality…

A nailbiting thriller from award-winning Malorie Blackman.

'One of today's outstandingly imaginative and convincing writers' *Junior Bookshelf*

'A whodunnit, a cyber-thriller and a family drama' *The Sunday Times*

'Lots of pacy action and snappy dialogue' *Daily Telegraph*

ISBN 0 552 528404